FLYING

BY GAIL GIBBONS

HOLIDAY HOUSE   NEW YORK

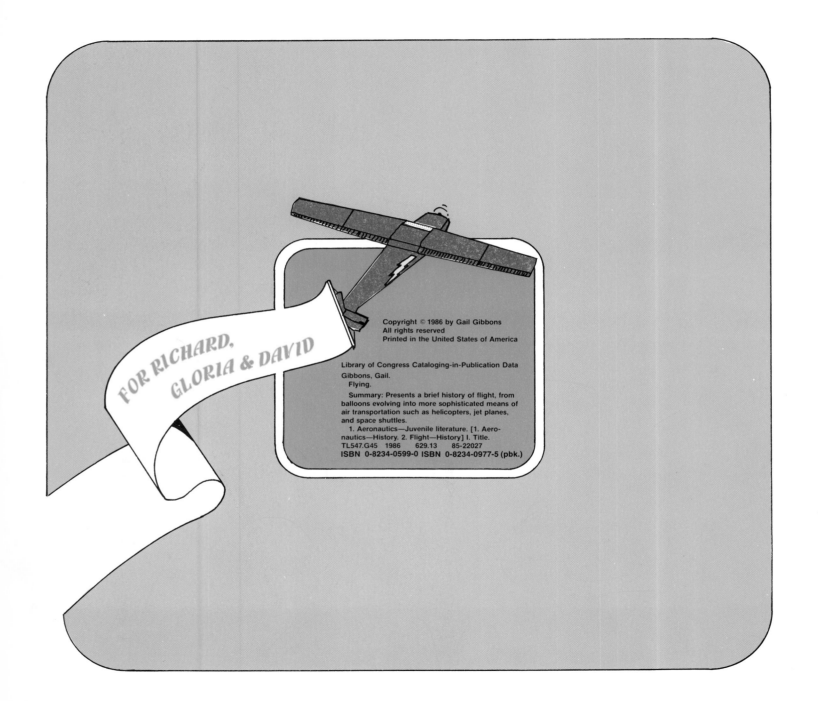

FOR RICHARD, GLORIA & DAVID

Library of Congress Cataloging-in-Publication Data
Gibbons, Gail.
  Flying.
  Summary: Presents a brief history of flight, from
balloons evolving into more sophisticated means of
air transportation such as helicopters, jet planes,
and space shuttles.
  1. Aeronautics—Juvenile literature. [1. Aeronautics—History. 2. Flight—History] I. Title.
TL547.G45 1986   629.13   85-22027
ISBN 0-8234-0599-0 ISBN 0-8234-0977-5 (pbk.)

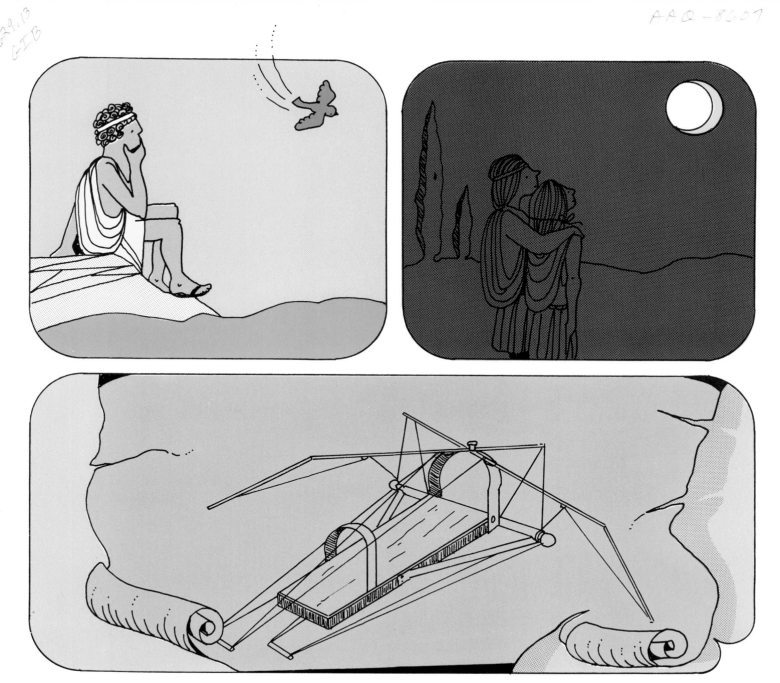

People have always wanted to fly.

**Years ago the first balloon to carry passengers was
tested in France. It carried a duck, a rooster and
a sheep, and they all landed safely.**

A few months later the two balloon inventors went up in the air.

Next, balloons that could be steered, called dirigibles, were seen. They were also called airships.

At the same time attempts were made to use wings for flying.

Finally, the Wright Brothers succeeded in flying a plane for the first time. The plane they built flew for only 12 seconds.

Just two years later another plane of theirs stayed up in the air for 30 minutes.

Today balloons are used for sport and...

for weather forecasting.

**Blimps are sometimes seen floating over sporting events.
Television cameras get a bird's-eye view of the game.**

Winged aircraft are seen, too.
There are hang gliders.

A sailplane, also called a glider, is towed up and released to soar before returning to the ground.

propeller

There are small planes with propellers. Their engines turn the propellers to make them go.

Some are flown for fun.

The view is different from above.

Some do fancy stunts and . . .

others write messages.

Other propeller planes do work, too.

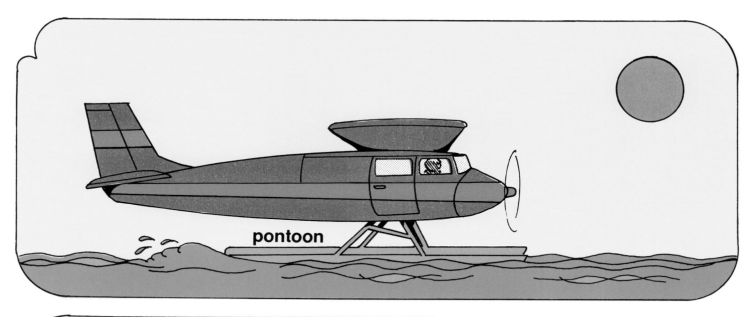

pontoon

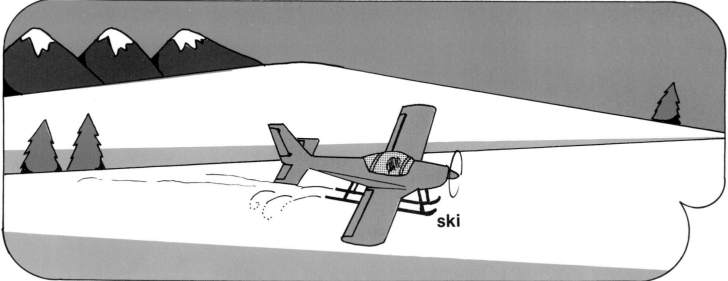

ski

Planes with pontoons land on water.
Planes with skiis land on snow.

rotor

Aircraft with propellers on their tops are called helicopters. The propellers are actually rotating wings called rotors. Helicopters can fly straight up and sideways, as well as forward.

They are used to do many different things.

Jet planes are fast. They can be small . . .

jet engines

or big. Their powerful engines push them forward.

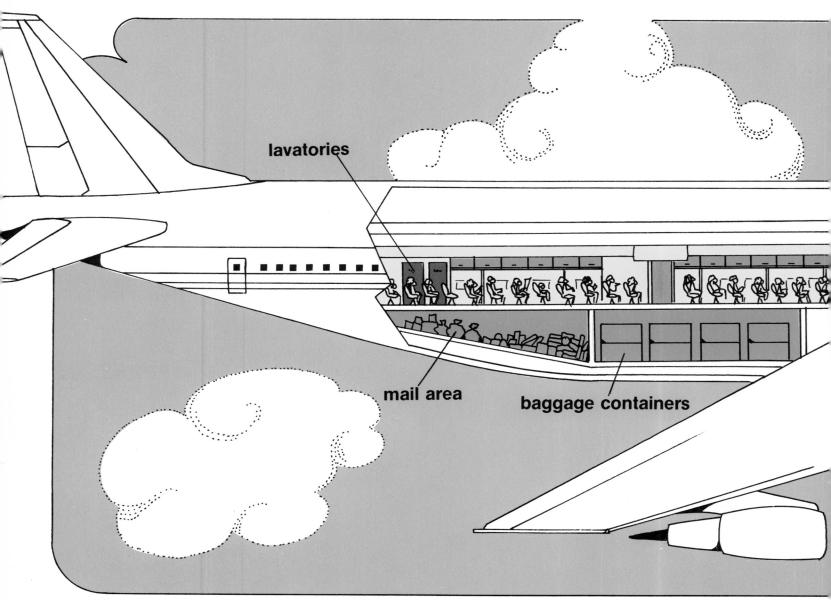

lavatories

mail area

baggage containers

Some jets carry passengers to different cities and countries.

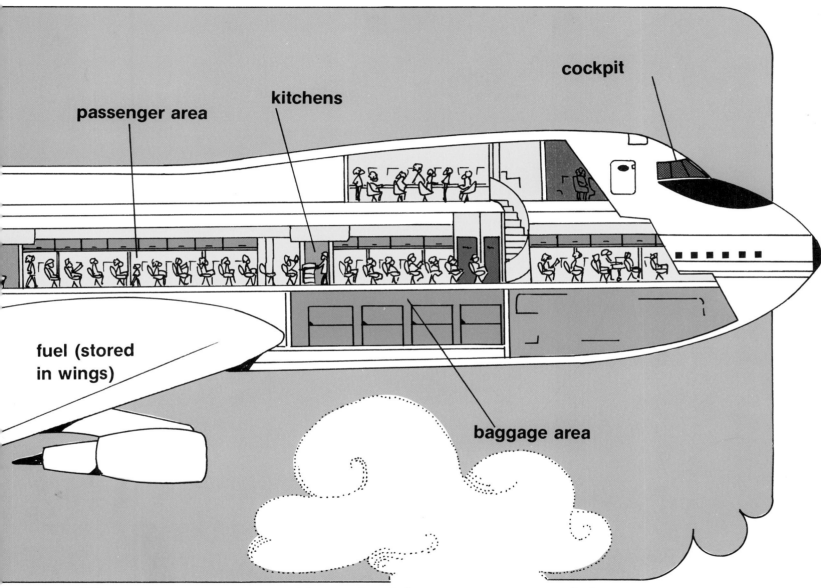

passenger area

kitchens

cockpit

fuel (stored in wings)

baggage area

There are many sections inside a passenger jet.

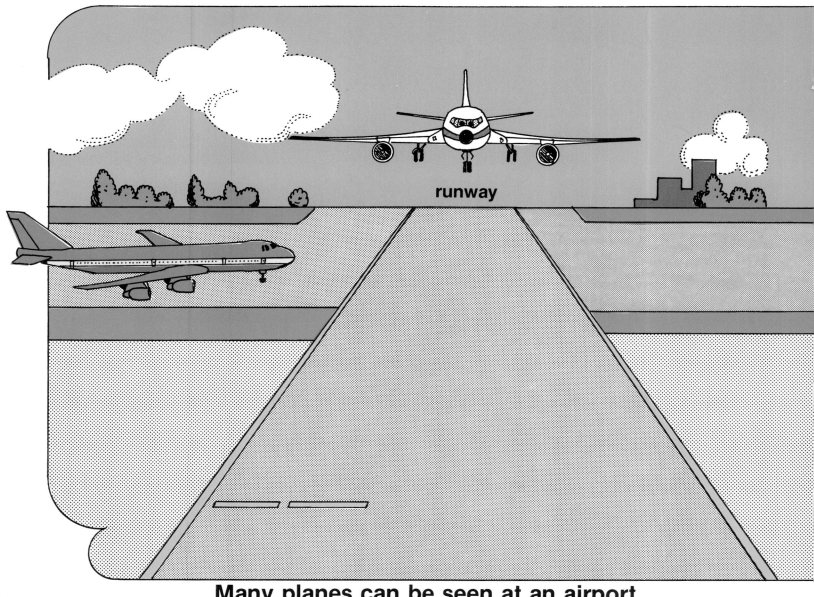

runway

Many planes can be seen at an airport.
It is a very busy place.

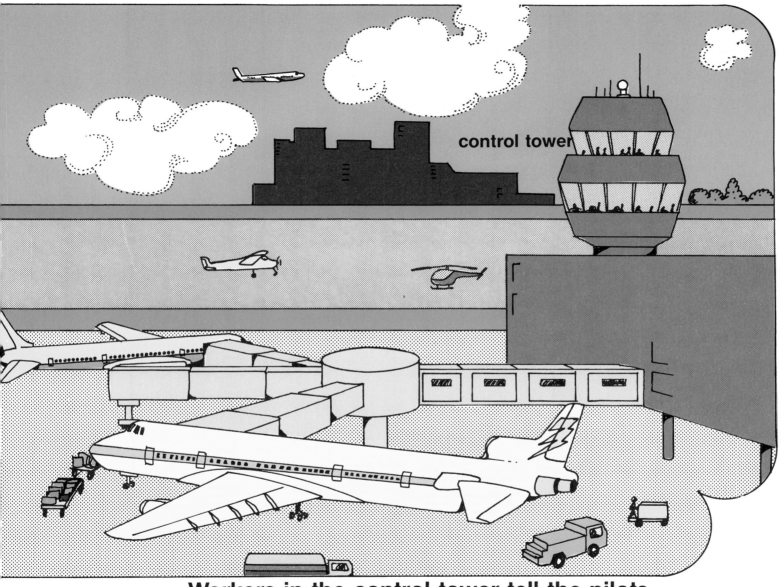

control tower

Workers in the control tower tell the pilots when they can take off and land.

Rockets have taken people into outer space and back in a capsule.

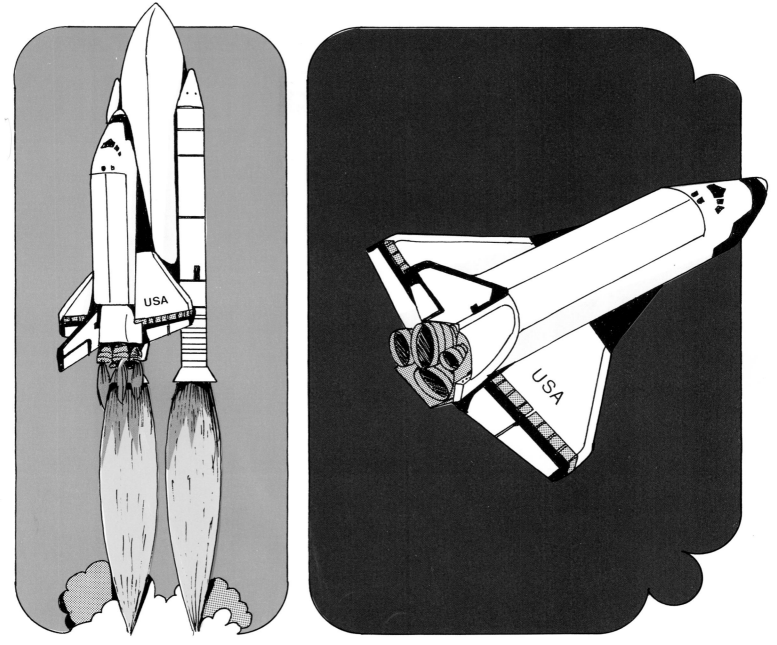

Now people fly into space and back in a space shuttle.

FAMOUS FLIGHTS

1783
The first manned balloon flight took place in France.

1903
The Wright Brothers flew a plane for the first time, in Kitty Hawk, North Carolina.

1926
Admiral Richard Byrd and Floyd Bennett were the first people to fly a plane over the North Pole.

1927
Charles Lindbergh, in his plane *The Spirit of St. Louis*, was the first person to fly alone across the Atlantic Ocean.

1947
Chuck Yeager was the first to break the sound barrier. His plane flew 670 miles an hour.

1962
John Glenn was the first American to orbit the Earth.

1969
Neil Armstrong was the first person to set foot on the moon.

1981
Columbia flew the first successful space shuttle mission.

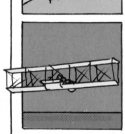